For Miguel
—BJH

tiger tales
an imprint of ME Media, LLC
202 Old Ridgefield Road, Wilton, CT 06897
Published in the United States 2006
Originally published in Great Britain 2005
By Hutchinson
An imprint of Random House Children's Books
Text copyright ©2005 Barbara Jean Hicks
Illustrations copyright ©2005 Lila Prap
CIP data is available
ISBN 1-58925-057-5
Printed in Singapore
1 3 5 7 9 10 8 6 4 2

I Like
Colors

by Barbara Jean Hicks

Illustrated by Lila Prap

tiger tales

wacky

quacky

quick

and slow

friendly

and low

striped

and spotted

shallow

deep

quiet

loud

awake

asleep

short

and tall

a lot

a few

enough for me . . .

enough

for you!

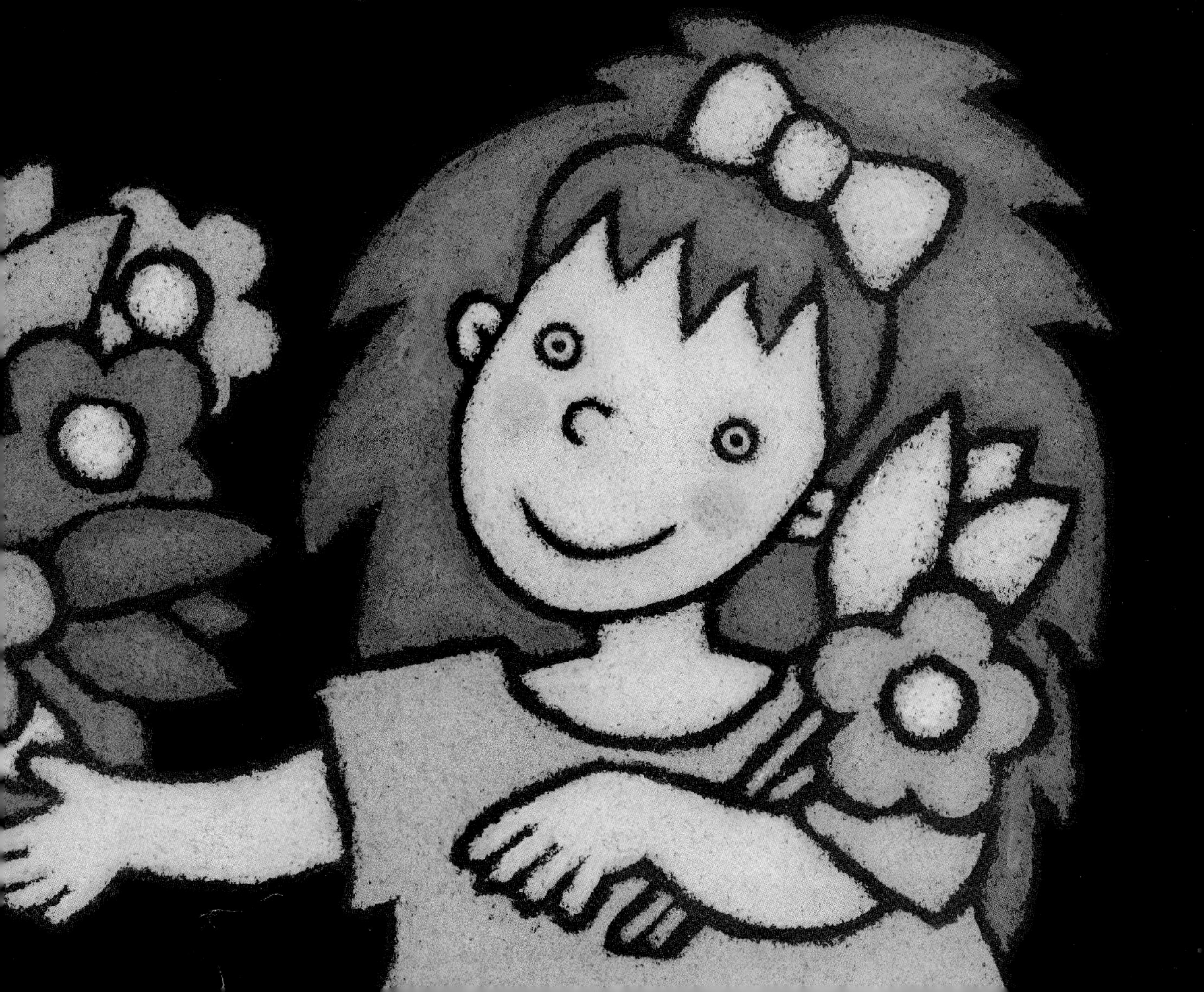

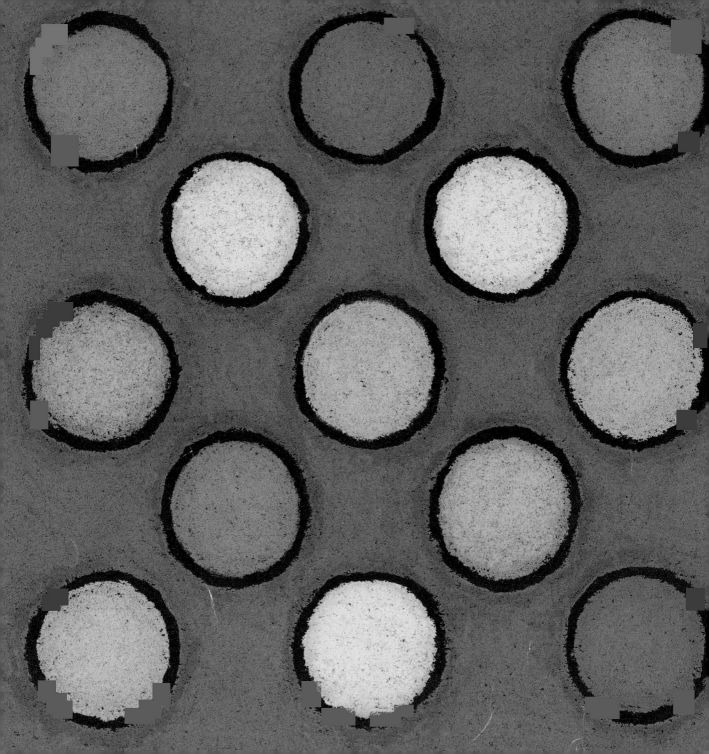